WELCOME TO
PASSPORT TO READING
A beginning reader's ticket to a brand-new world!

Every book in this program is designed to build read-along and read-alone skills, level by level, through engaging and enriching stories. As the reader turns each page, he or she will become more confident with new vocabulary, sight words, and comprehension.

These PASSPORT TO READING levels will help you choose the perfect book for every reader.

READING TOGETHER
Read short words in simple sentence structures together to begin a reader's journey.

READING OUT LOUD
Encourage developing readers to sound out words in more complex stories with simple vocabulary.

READING INDEPENDENTLY
Newly independent readers gain confidence reading more complex sentences with higher word counts.

READY TO READ MORE
Readers prepare for chapter books with fewer illustrations and longer paragraphs.

This book features sight words from the educator-supported Dolch Sight Words List. This encourages the reader to recognize commonly used vocabulary words, increasing reading speed and fluency.

For more information, please visit www.passporttoreadingbooks.com.

Enjoy the journey!

To Nicole

Little, Brown and Company

Hachette Book Group
237 Park Avenue, New York, NY 10017
Visit our website at www.lb-kids.com

Little, Brown and Company is a division of Hachette Book Group, Inc.
The Little, Brown name and logo are trademarks of Hachette Book Group, Inc.

The publisher is not responsible for websites (or their content) that are not owned by the publisher.

Abridged Edition: September 2013
First published in hardcover in April 1980 by Little, Brown and Company

Library of Congress Cataloging-in-Publication Data

Christopher, Matt.
The dog that stole football plays / by Matt Christopher ; illustrated by Steve Björkman. — Abridged edition.
pages cm. — (Passport to reading. Level 3)
"First published in...1980 by Little, Brown and Company"—Copyright page.
Summary: A boy and his psychic dog are able to steal plays from the opposing football team.
ISBN 978-0-316-21849-8
[1. Dogs—Fiction. 2. Extrasensory perception—Fiction. 3. Football—Fiction.] I. Björkman, Steve, illustrator.
II. Title.
PZ7.C458Do 2013
[E]—dc23

2012047508

10 9 8 7 6 5 4 3 2 1

IM

Printed in Malaysia

Passport to Reading titles are leveled by independent reviewers applying the standards developed by Irene Fountas and Gay Su Pinnell in *Matching Books to Readers: Using Leveled Books in Guided Reading*, Heinemann, 1999.

The Dog That Stole Football Plays

by **MATT CHRISTOPHER**
illustrated by **Steve Björkman**

LITTLE, BROWN AND COMPANY
New York   Boston

Mike and his dog, Harry, shared a secret.

They could speak to each other with their minds!

Mike first saw Harry in an animal shelter.

He was shocked that he could understand the

dog's thoughts, and the dog could understand his!

It was the start of one of the best friendships ever.

Mike played football for a team called the Jets.

One night, Harry asked, "Hey, Mike, when are you

going to take me to a practice or game?"

"Harry, you would just be in the way," Mike said.

"No, I would not.

You will be surprised when you see

how much I can help you," said Harry.

Mike did not think Harry would be of any help at all,

but he brought him to the first game of the year.

The Jets were playing the Rams.

Harry sat near the other team's bench

and listened.

"Jones, take the ball and go over left tackle,"

he heard the coach say.

"Mike, watch for Jones going over left tackle,"

Harry thought.

Mike followed the directions

and made the tackle on the field.

The Rams did not gain a yard.

"Yeah, Mike!" the fans cheered.

During the third quarter,

the Rams moved the ball

to the Jets' twenty-eight-yard line.

It was tense.

A message from Harry came into

Mike's thoughts.

"Thirty-two.

Run through right tackle."

Mike smiled.

"Okay, guys," he said to his teammates.

"A run through right tackle!

Cover that hole!"

When the Rams halfback tried to bust

through his right-tackle side,

he did not gain an inch.

In fact, he *lost* a yard.

Another message came from Harry.

"Fourteen!

Long pass down the right corner."

Mike looked at Butch.

"Watch for a long pass

down in your corner, Butch," he said.

Butch intercepted the ball!

In two plays, the Jets scored a touchdown.

The Jets won the game with a score of 28–7.

Harry really helped!

But Mike wondered if using Harry was fair.

"Are we cheating, Harry?" Mike asked.

Harry gave a short bark.

"Why ask me?" he replied.

"I am just a dog.

If you do not want to hear the plays,

that is fine with me."

Mike was confused.

He decided to think about it later.

After the Jets' fourth win,

Mike's father took the whole team out

for hamburgers.

Curly Lucas was the captain of the Tigers team.

He came over to talk to Mike.

"We are playing you guys next week," said Curly.

"How about the losers buy the winners hamburgers?"

"Sounds great!" exclaimed Mike.

With Harry giving him the plays,

he knew the Jets would beat the Tigers.

But on Saturday morning before the game,

Harry was sick!

"It must have been that old bone I found in

the yard," Harry groaned.

"I just cannot make it today."

"Oh no!" cried Mike.

But the game had to go on

with or without Harry.

The Tigers scored a touchdown in the first

five minutes of the game.

Mike saw Curly's big smile.

He knew Curly was already thinking

about his hamburger.

Before the quarter ended,

the Tigers were up, 14–0.

"You were crazy to take Curly up on that bet," Butch said, glaring at Mike.

"Those Tigers are just too big for us, and your magic—or whatever it is—is not working."

"I am sorry," said Mike.

"Why did that dumb dog have to get sick now?" he thought.

At halftime, Mike sat on the bench.

Mike's father came over.

"Giving up?" he asked.

"Dad!" cried Mike.

"They are bigger than we are!"

"So what?

Take them down to your size," said his father.

Mike thought for a minute.

"You are right, Dad," he said.

"Even if they are bigger,

we can give them a good fight!"

Mike jumped off the bench

with his heart full of hope.

The Jets were like a new team.

They ran harder.

They tackled better.

They blocked.

They knocked down passes.

Soon they were only one touchdown

behind the Tigers.

When the second half was almost over,

Butch shouted to Mike, "Your dog, Harry,

just came into the park!

Maybe he will bring us good luck."

Mike's heart leaped.

"Oh, good!

He is okay!" he cried.

"But we are doing all right without him."

"What?" asked Butch, staring at him.

Mike sent a message to Harry asking him

to keep quiet for the rest of the game.

"Hey, guys!" he cried.

"How about we give those Tigers a fight?

Show them we are more than small guys!

Show them we have guts!"

"Okay!" Mike said to himself.

"We are going to win without Harry."

The Jets continued to play tough ball

and scored another touchdown.

When the final whistle blew,

the game was tied, 21–21.

After the game, Mike bought an extra

hamburger for Harry.

"This is a special reward for you,"

he told the dog.

"You have been talking funny all day,"

said Butch.

"So would you," said Mike,

"if you had a dog like Harry.

Right, Harry?"

"Woof!" said Harry.